Copyright © 1997 by Nord-Süd Verlag AG, Gossau Zürich, Switzerland.
First published in Switzerland under the title *Die fünf Finger und der Mond*.
English translation copyright © 1997 by North-South Books Inc.

All rights reserved.
No part of this book may be reproduced or utilized in any form
or by any means, electronic or mechanical, including photocopying,
recording, or any information storage and retrieval system,
without permission in writing from the publisher.

First published in the United States, Great Britain, Canada,
Australia, and New Zealand in 1997 by North-South Books,
an imprint of Nord-Süd Verlag AG, Gossau Zürich, Switzerland.

Library of Congress Cataloging-in-Publication Data is available.
A CIP catalogue record for this book is available from The British Library.
ISBN 1-55858-801-9 (trade binding)
1 3 5 7 9 TB 10 8 6 4 2
ISBN 1-55858-802-7 (library binding)
1 3 5 7 9 LB 10 8 6 4 2
Printed in Belgium

For more information about our books, and the authors and artists
who create them, visit our web site: http://www.northsouth.com

The Five Fingers and the Moon

By Kemal Kurt

Illustrated by Aljoscha Blau

Translated by Anthea Bell

North-South Books

New York · London

Far away, beyond the edge of the horizon, the Queen of Elsewhere lived happily with her subjects: dwarves, brownies, fairies, elves, and many other creatures who have no place in our own world.

Time passed in Elsewhere just as it passes here on Earth. Day followed night, there were four seasons, Elsewhere moved around the sun, and the moon moved around Elsewhere. However, the people of Elsewhere slept by day and lived their lives by night, working, playing, eating, singing, and making merry after the sun went down. Most nights the moon shone down on them, sometimes big and round like the lid of a pan, sometimes thin and curved as a sickle. Sometimes it did not shine at all, but the brownies, dwarves, and fairies knew that their beloved moon was only resting and would soon be back.

One night, when the moon was nearly but not quite full, it suddenly stopped moving across the sky.

The Queen and all the people of Elsewhere were alarmed, for the rising and setting of the moon ruled their lives. If the moon stood still, the grass and the grain would stop growing, and so would the dwarves' beards. The cows would not give milk. The fairies' songs would fall silent, and the brownies would play no games in the woods at night.

So the Queen summoned her Seven Counsellors to decide what to do. They were all very wise, and they were all very old, too.

"The moon is standing still in the sky because part of it has come loose and fallen to the ground," said the wisest dwarf. "We must help the poor moon."

"But how?" asked the Queen in despair.

'There's nothing the five fingers of the hand can't do," said an old fairy with a bent back. "Let's ask them for help."

So first the Queen sent for the thumb. "Thumbkin," she said, "you are strong, and lucky, too. We want you to give this back to the moon." She handed him the fallen crescent of moon.

Thumbkin had often helped to move a rock blocking a mountain road, or a tree blown down in a storm, but this was a much more difficult problem.

Holding the bright crescent, Thumbkin climbed the highest mountain in Elsewhere. All the people gathered at the foot of the mountain, watching, while the moon looked down from above. They crossed their fingers.

Thumbkin took a running start and tried to throw the crescent up to the moon. But it fell short, and came flying back like a boomerang. Thumbkin caught it in midair. The people of Elsewhere groaned with disappointment.

On his second attempt, the crescent only just missed the moon, and when he tried for a third time, it sailed up to the moon, landing right in the exact place where it had been before it fell.

The moon was whole again, so at last it could set.

The next day the people of Elsewhere slept soundly again.

The following evening, however, they realized that there was still a teeny, tiny piece missing from the moon. Where could it be?

Chimney sweeps poked their long brushes down chimneys, foresters searched the mossy woodland floor, divers went down to the bottom of the sea, but no one could find the missing piece of moon.

"The Lord of Darkness must have hidden it," said the wisest Counsellor. "He hates to see light in Elsewhere by night. Remember the eclipse not long ago? That was his doing. He hung his black cloak over the moon."

They all remembered. Forty oxen had spent hours tugging at the edges of the black cloak until at last they dragged it off, and then two hundred dwarves had worked busily cutting the cloak into pieces, which they hid in dark caves.

"Now the Lord of Darkness has stolen that piece of the moon," declared the wise old dwarf. "We need a master thief to steal it back."

"Let's call in thieving Pointer!" the other Counsellors cried. They meant Pointer the forefinger, who was known far and wide for his habit of dipping into everything.

The Queen's messengers found him in the good fairy's larder, eating honey from a big green bowl. Caught red-handed, Pointer felt so guilty that he agreed to try to steal back the little piece of moon.

Pointer searched and searched for it, far beyond the mountains, and at last, quite by chance, his own greed led him to the right place. Feeling hungry, he shook a plum tree, and several plums fell into the well below. When he looked into the water, he saw a faint light. The Lord of Darkness had hidden the piece of moon there, weighting it down with a rock. Pointer climbed down the well, pushed the heavy rock aside, and set the piece of moon free.

Then Thumbkin easily threw it back to its old place once more.

Now the moon was full again, but it stayed full and would not wax and wane.

Night after night, the wolves howled at the full moon. High tides flooded the land. Everyone in Elsewhere worried.

There was only one person who might be able to reach the moon and get it moving again: Long Man, the middle finger. He was the tallest person in Elsewhere, so the Queen summoned him to court.

Long Man was tall and thin, and he wore a full suit of mail. Kissing the hem of the Queen's cloak, he thanked her for her faith in him.

After much thought, Long Man came up with an idea. He had all the ladders in Elsewhere taken to the top of the highest mountain in the land. The brownies tied the ladders together, and everyone helped raise them to the moon. Very carefully Long Man put his foot on the bottom rung.

The people of Elsewhere held their breath, hoping the wind would not blow, for that would be the end of poor Long Man.

Rung by rung Long Man climbed the ladder, pausing several times to wait for it to stop shaking. The brownies, fairies, and dwarves watched in suspense as he stepped very, very cautiously onto the top rung. Then he stretched, and sure enough, he could touch the moon. Standing on tiptoe, he took the outer crescent of the moon away and climbed down again. The crowd clapped and cheered as he set foot on the ground once more.

But the moon still could not wax and wane on its own, and the Queen and her subjects were in despair. Something must be done! The Seven Counsellors suggested sending Gold Man, the ring finger, to try to cure the moon once and for all. Gold Man was famous far beyond the land of Elsewhere as a healer.

The Master of the Queen's Fireworks worked all night making two rockets. The next evening, they all climbed the mountain: The Queen led the way, together with Gold Man, the Master of the Fireworks and his assistants, and everyone else. The Master fastened one of the rockets to Gold Man's back. Gold Man was nervous about this idea, but he didn't want to look like a coward, so he took his doctor's bag in one hand and the rocket for the return journey in the other, and they shot him off.

The Master of the Fireworks had taken good aim. The flight went well, and soon Gold Man landed on the moon and began to examine his patient.

He took away another little piece to make the moon smaller again; then he greased and oiled all its joints so that it could move smoothly.

When Gold Man had finished, he tied the second rocket to his back and flew home. Now the moon was cured and could turn again, waxing and waning properly.

There was great rejoicing in Elsewhere. The Queen declared three days of celebration, and long tables were laid with a delicious feast. Strong Thumbkin and greedy Pointer sat on one side of the Queen at the banquet; tall Long Man and Gold Man the doctor sat on her other side.

And what about Pinkie, the little finger? This was his moment. A clever, merry little fellow, Pinkie was the only person in Elsewhere who could count to five and make up songs at any time.

So Pinkie strummed his lute and sang a song in praise of the five fingers of the hand, who can do anything if they really want to.